DREAMWORKS

DRAGONS

How to Start a
DRAGON
ACADEMY

adapted by Erica David

Ready-to-Read

Simon Spotlight

New York   London   Toronto   Sydney   New Delhi

SIMON SPOTLIGHT

An imprint of Simon & Schuster Children's Publishing Division

1230 Avenue of the Americas, New York, New York 10020

First Simon Spotlight edition August 2014

DreamWorks Dragons: Riders of Berk © 2014 DreamWorks Animation L.L.C.

All rights reserved, including the right of reproduction in whole or in part in any form.

SIMON SPOTLIGHT, READY-TO-READ, and colophon are registered trademarks of Simon & Schuster, Inc.

For information about special discounts for bulk purchases, please contact

Simon & Schuster Special Sales at 1-866-506-1949 or business@simonandschuster.com.

The Simon & Schuster Speakers Bureau can bring authors to your live event.

For more information or to book an event contact the Simon & Schuster Speakers Bureau at

1-866-248-3049 or visit our website at www.simonspeakers.com.

Manufactured in the United States of America 0714 LAK

2 4 6 8 10 9 7 5 3 1

ISBN 978-1-4814-1926-0 (hc)

ISBN 978-1-4814-1925-3 (pbk)

ISBN 978-1-4814-1927-7 (eBook)

Vikings and dragons
used to be enemies.
Then Hiccup met his dragon, Toothless.
They became best friends.

Now Vikings and dragons
live side by side on Berk.

Most Vikings are happy to share
their home with dragons.
But sometimes the dragons
get into trouble.

The dragons scare fish
out of the Vikings' nets.
They chase sheep out of their pens.
And they steal food.

Usually the Vikings
can forgive the dragons.
But some Vikings are angry
when the dragons eat their food.
They are trying to store food
for the winter freeze that is coming.

There is one Viking named Mildew
who is very upset.
The dragons ate his entire field of
cabbage!

"Stoick, you need to put those dragons in cages!" Mildew shouts. "If you don't, they will eat us out of house and home!"

"They don't mean any harm,"
Hiccup replies.
"They are just dragons being dragons."
Chief Stoick tells Mildew
he will handle the dragons.

That night Hiccup asks Stoick if he
can help with the dragons.
"You?" Stoick asks.
"If anyone can control them,
I can," Hiccup says.
Stoick decides to give Hiccup a chance.

The next day Hiccup and Toothless
go to the village square.
Hiccup feels confident that he can
get the dragons under control.

The dragons are up to
their usual tricks.
Hiccup watches as a Deadly Nadder
sneaks up to a house to
steal a loaf of bread.

Hiccup chases after the Nadder and places a hand on his nose. "No!" Hiccup says firmly.

The Deadly Nadder listens
and drops the bread.

But while Hiccup is training
one dragon, other dragons
make trouble all over the village.
Hiccup tries to stop them
but it is no use.
It begins to look like he is helping
the dragons break things!

Hiccup realizes he cannot
train the dragons alone.

The next day Hiccup invites his
friends and their dragons to the arena.
"The dragons are out of control,"
he says. "We want them
to live in our world
without destroying it, but
they can't without our help."

Hiccup shows his friends
how to scratch under a dragon's
chin to get it to drop stolen food.

It seems like they are making progress.
But when they head into the village
to find dragons to train,
there are no dragons in sight.